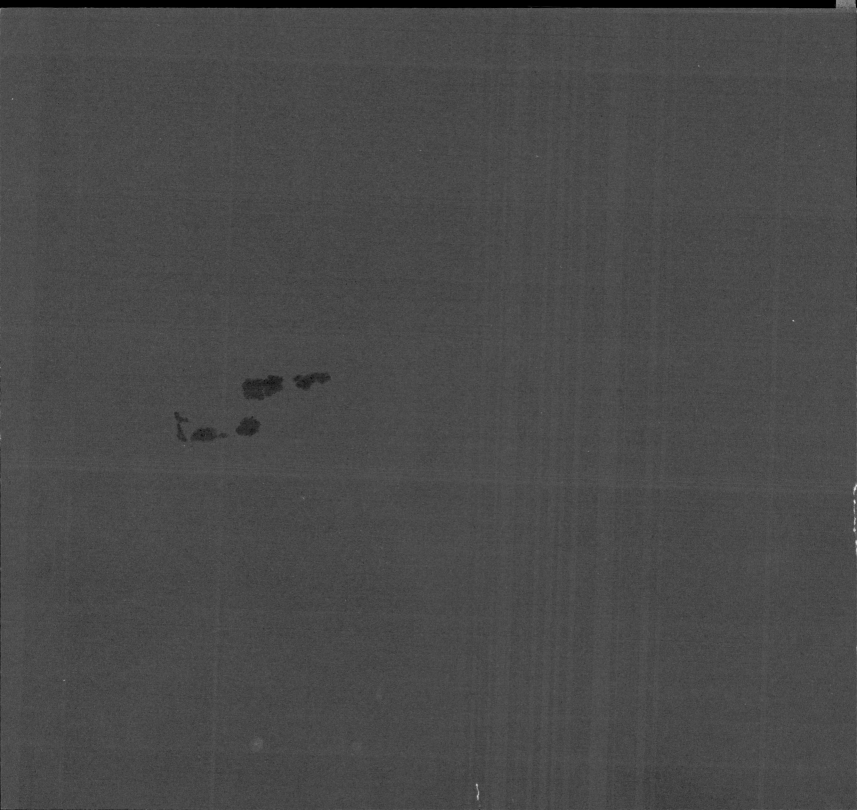

Good King Wenceslas

ILLUSTRATED BY JOHN WALLNER

Philomel Books • New York

22901

Good King Wenceslas, a tenth century duke and patron saint of
Bohemia, was noted for his piety and hard work to strengthen Christianity
in the kingdom of Bohemia, now a province of Czechoslovakia.

Illustrations copyright © 1990 by John Wallner
Musical arrangement copyright © 1987 by Susan Friedlander
Published by Philomel Books, a division of The Putnam & Grosset Book Group,
200 Madison Avenue, New York, NY 10016. Published simultaneously
in Canada. All rights reserved. Printed in Hong Kong
by South China Printing Co. (1988) Ltd. Book design by Golda Laurens

Library of Congress Cataloging-in-Publication Data
Wallner, John C.   Good King Wenceslas: a picture book/
illustrated by John Wallner. p. cm.
Summary: a retelling of the old song of the good king
who went out into the countryside at Christmas time to share
with the poor. Includes music.   1. Carols, English—Texts.
2. Christmas music.   [1. Carols, English   2. Christmas music.]   I. Title.
PZ8.3.W185Go 1990 782.28'1723'0268—dc20 89-26640 CIP AC
ISBN 0-399-21620-0
First impression

I wish you the golden gift of Wenceslas:
that you may come to the edge of the forest
and reach out your hand in peace and receive friendship.

—J.W.

Good King Wenceslas look'd out, on the Feast of Stephen,

When the snow lay round about, deep and crisp and even;

Brightly shone the moon that night, tho' the frost was cruel,

When a poor man came in sight, gath'ring winter fuel.

"Hither, page, and stand by me, if thou know'st it telling;

Yonder peasant, who is he? Where, and what his dwelling?"

"Sire, he lives a good league hence, underneath the mountain;

Right against the forest fence, by Saint Agnes' fountain."

"Bring me flesh and bring me wine, bring me pine logs hither;

Thou and I will see him dine when we bear them thither."

Page and monarch forth they went, forth they went together;

Thro' the rude wind's wild lament and the bitter weather.

"Sire, the night is darker now, and the wind blows stronger;

Fails my heart, I know not how, I can go no longer."

"Mark my footsteps, my good page, tread thou in them boldly:

Thou shalt find the winter's rage freeze thy blood less coldly."

In his master's steps he trod, where the snow lay dinted;

Heat was in the very sod which the saint had printed;

Therefore, Christian men, be sure, wealth or rank possessing,

Ye who now will bless the poor, shall yourselves find blessing.

GOOD KING WENCESLAS

John Mason Neale

Traditional
Arranged by Sir John Stainer

Robustly

1. Good King Wen - ces - las look'd out On the Feast of Steph - en, When the snow lay
2. "Hith - er, page, and stand by me, If thou know'st it, tell - ing; Yon - der peas - ant,
3. "Bring me flesh, and bring me wine, Bring me pine - logs hith - er; Thou and I will
4. "Sire, the night is dark - er now, And the wind blows strong - er; Fails my heart, I
5. In his mas - ter's steps he trod, Where the snow lay dint - ed; Heat was in the

round a - bout, Deep and crisp and e - ven; Bright - ly shone the moon that night, Tho' the frost was
who is he? Where, and what his dwell - ing?" "Sire, he lives a good league hence, Un - der - neath the
see him dine When we bear them thith - er." Page and mon - arch forth they went, Forth they went to -
know not how, I can go no long - er." "Mark my foot - steps, my good page, Tread thou in them
ver - y sod Which the saint had print - ed; There - fore, Chris - tian men, be sure, Wealth or rank pos -

cru - el, When a poor man came in sight, Gath - 'ring win - ter fu - el.
moun - tain; Right a - gainst the for - est fence, By Saint Ag - nes' foun - tain."
geth - er; Thro' the rude wind's wild la - ment And the bit - ter weath - er.
bold - ly: Thou shalt find the win - ter's rage Freeze thy blood less cold - ly."
ses - sing, Ye who now will bless the poor, Shall your - selves find bless - ing.